THIS BOOK BELONGS TO

_____

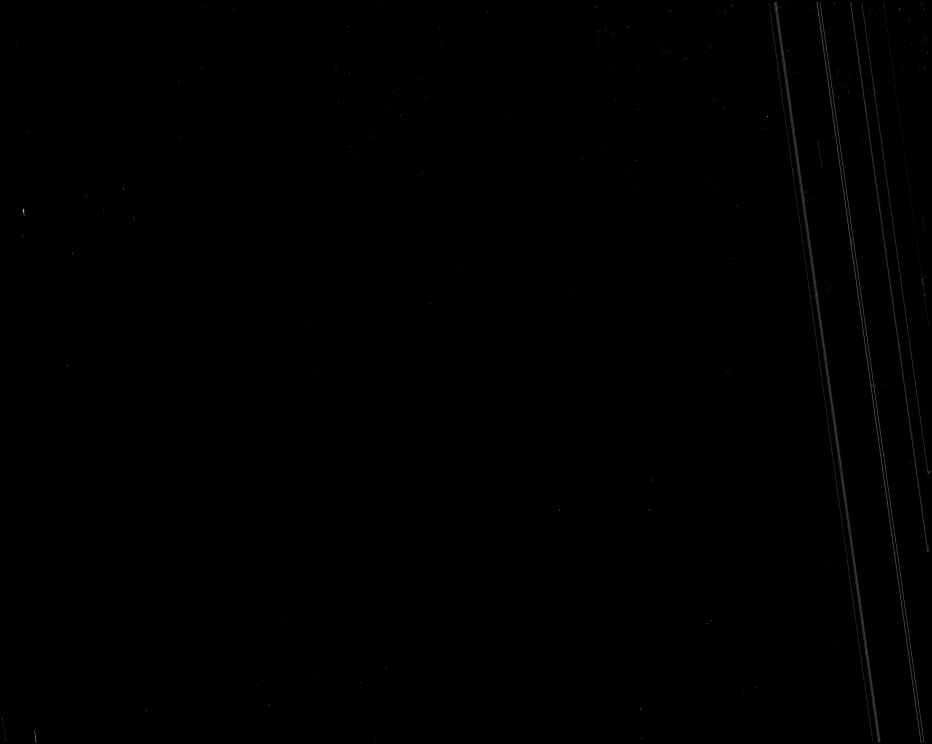

PEANUTS
The Great Pumpkin
RETURNS

By Charles M. Schulz
Adapted by Jason Cooper
Illustrated by Scott Jeralds

Simon Spotlight
New York London Toronto Sydney New Delhi

SIMON SPOTLIGHT
An imprint of Simon & Schuster Children's Publishing Division
1230 Avenue of the Americas, New York, New York 10020
First Simon Spotlight edition July 2017

SIMON SPOTLIGHT and colophon are registered trademarks of Simon & Schuster, Inc. For information about special discounts for bulk purchases, please contact Simon & Schuster Special Sales at 1-866-506-1949 or business@simonandschuster.com. Manufactured in China 0517 LEO
10 9 8 7 6 5 4 3 2 1   ISBN 978-1-4814-9664-3   ISBN 978-1-4814-9665-0 (eBook)

Every fall, while all the kids in the neighborhood pick out their Halloween costumes, Linus Van Pelt sits at home and writes a very important letter.

Dear Great Pumpkin, I am looking forward to your arrival on Halloween night. I will be waiting for you, as usual, in my pumpkin patch. . . .

Unfortunately, not everyone believes in the Great Pumpkin. Linus's sister, Lucy, is one of those people.

"Don't tell me you're writing another letter to that ridiculous fruit," Lucy says. "You're the only person in the whole world who believes in that fairy tale. There's no such thing as the Great Pumpkin!"

Linus thinks Lucy is wrong. "He's not a fairy tale! He's real!" he tells her. Then Linus gets an idea. "I'll show you," says Linus. "I'll find someone else who believes in the Great Pumpkin, and on Halloween night, we'll wait in the pumpkin patch together."

Linus asks Sally if she would like to wait with him for the Great Pumpkin's return.

"Not again!" Sally says. "Fool me once, shame on you. Fool me twice, and I sue."

Linus asks other friends but is surprised to learn none of them believe in the Great Pumpkin. Not Franklin. Not Pigpen. Not Marcie.

"Sorry, Linus. I just don't believe in the Great Grape," Marcie says.

Not even Linus's best friend, good ol' Charlie Brown, believes.

"Come on, Charlie Brown. You believe in the Great Pumpkin, don't you?" Linus asks.

Charlie Brown appreciates that this is very important to Linus, but he has to be honest. "Well . . . ," says Charlie Brown, "I believe that *you* believe in the Great Pumpkin. Does that help at all?"

Linus feels defeated.

"No one believes in the Great Pumpkin," Linus complains to his friend Peppermint Patty.

"What's a Great Pumpkin?" Peppermint Patty asks.

Linus's eyes light up! "Every Halloween night, the Great Pumpkin arises majestically from a sincere pumpkin patch and showers his believers with presents and warm autumn wishes!" he explains.

"Really?" asks Peppermint Patty.

"Yes! Warm autumn wishes!" Linus repeats.

"And presents?" Peppermint Patty asks.

"Fabulous presents!" Linus tells her. "But you must have faith and accept his presents with a pure heart and deep sense of gratitude."

"I can do that!" shouts Peppermint Patty.

Peppermint Patty shakes Linus's hand excitedly. "That sounds fantastic! Count me in. If there are presents, then I believe in the Great Pumpkin too," she says.

The day before Halloween, Marcie asks Peppermint Patty for advice.
"What costume should I wear, sir? Astronaut or restaurant critic?"
"You can never go wrong with circus clown," says Peppermint Patty.
"What will you be wearing?" Marcie asks.
"I'm not trick-or-treating this year," Peppermint Patty announces. "I'm
waiting for the Great Pumpkin with Linus!"

Marcie thinks Peppermint Patty is making a bad decision. "Don't do that, sir! The Great Zucchini isn't real!"

"Pumpkin," corrects Peppermint Patty. "I believe in him. I even wrote him a letter. As for trick-or-treating, I'll just send my Halloween candy bag with you. You can drop it off for me when it's full."

At last it's Halloween night. Linus is waiting patiently in the pumpkin patch when he sees two familiar faces—Snoopy and Woodstock!

"Are you waiting for the Great Pumpkin too?" Linus asks.

Snoopy shakes his head no. *Sorry, old sport, we must be going,* Snoopy thinks, patting Linus on the back. *We're on a top secret mission!*

Woodstock chirps in excitement.

Snoopy continues his thought. *That's right—that house over there is giving out homemade popcorn balls!*

Peppermint Patty finally arrives at the pumpkin patch. "When's this Great Pumpkin guy supposed to show up?" she asks.

"Who knows? That's part of the fun!" cheers Linus.

"Well, I'll wait as long as I have to, just so long as I get my new baseball glove," says Peppermint Patty. "That's what I asked the Great Pumpkin to bring me."

Linus is shocked. "You can't ask for something specific!" he says. "The Great Pumpkin brings whatever he chooses to bring you, if anything at all! He is benevolent and exercises his own judgment! You've insulted him! He's never going to show up now!"

"How was I supposed to know that?" Peppermint Patty hollers. "It's not like you gave me a brochure to read!"

Linus is furious. "Get out!" he says. "Leave this pumpkin patch!"

Linus looks to the sky and cries out, "Forgive me, Great Pumpkin! I didn't mean to insult you! Bring me whatever you want! Or don't! It's fine either way! Just show up this year . . . please. . . ."

An hour passes. Then another one. Linus wishes Peppermint Patty was still waiting with him. He feels embarrassed about insulting the Great Pumpkin and ashamed of how he treated his friend.

Linus is still in the pumpkin patch when Snoopy and Woodstock return. Snoopy is carrying a plate full of homemade popcorn balls.

Snoopy stops and gives Linus a popcorn ball. He thinks to himself, *Poor chap—looks like he's had a rough night. Have a treat. This mission was hard on us all.*

Snoopy and Woodstock march back home.

The next day, Linus bumps into Marcie, Charlie Brown, and Peppermint Patty. Linus looks at Peppermint Patty. "I'm sorry for how mean I was to you. I just wanted to see the Great Pumpkin so badly that I lost my temper."

"Don't feel bad, Linus," Peppermint Patty says. "There's always next year."

"It's always the same," complains Linus. "I wait and wait, and he never shows up. I should stop believing in the Great Pumpkin."

Marcie now understands how upset Linus is. "Don't stop believing," she tells him. "Your belief in the Great Pumpkin makes you a dreamer. The world needs dreamers."

Marcie's kindness makes Linus feel better.

"You're right! Next year I'll make that pumpkin patch even more sincere! Who's with me?" Linus asks.

"Not us," says Marcie. "But we are *behind* you."

"Last night wasn't all bad," Linus continues, thinking about it. "After all, Snoopy did bring me a popcorn ball!"

"You spent all night in a pumpkin patch and got a popcorn ball?" Charlie Brown sighs. "I went trick-or-treating for hours and only got a toothbrush!"